I HATE BOOKS

Rosiland Blanks

ISBN: 978-0-615-83517-4 (hardcover)

Dedicated
to my daughter,
Tyra Wallace.

Tomorrow is the first day of the school, I'm soooo geeked!

I wonder what the first grade will be like, will I meet new friends, have a great teacher, or just not like it at all. My mom called it the first day of the rest of my life, I call it one of the most exciting times of my life so far. While most kids my age where at the fun camps, on vacation, and playing sports all summer, I was at a reading camp reading a bunch of books and surrounded by a bunch of people I don't know. "Hi, my name is Jared and I hate books"!

Growing up as a young kid in a small town

called Roslyn in upper New York state I was always made to read. From the time I could understand what my mother was saying, she repeatedly said these words to me, "Jared, once you've read over a thousand books you will have the world at your fingertips". Ha! I bet that came from some book she once read. I live with my mother, father, and a bunch of books. My parents each have dark hair, and green eyes.

I was born with reddish hair, freckles, and brown eyes. Will someone please explain to me where the science in that comes from? Whenever I would play with the other kids, they would often tease me and tell me I spoke differently. Well, I do have a big vocabulary for a kid my age, from being forced to read all the time. "My name is Jared and boy do I hate books"!

My mother told me I began reading before I could walk. She also told me when I was younger, whenever we would go to the doctor's office, the other children would be playing with the table toys and building blocks, and I would be reading the newspaper, mainly the comic section. I often express my feelings about reading all the time, so she wonders why I hate reading so much. I think the best part of her day is trying to show me the joy of reading and all the different subjects I could read. I spend most of my day reading, morning, noon, and night; not much time for anything else. I read all kinds of books fantasies, biographies, mysteries, textbooks, non-fiction, science fiction, and just plain old fiction. In the morning's I would sit and read the newspaper with my dad before he's off to work. One day I decided to ask my mom if making me read brings her joy, then why she's not smiling. As she approached me with a serious look on her face, her response was, The day she notices that I enjoy reading, will be the day I will see her face will light up. Well, no light today I thought! Not seeing her smile was one of the worst parts of my day.

"My name is Jared, and I hate books".

My room is filled with bookshelves, there are so many books- like thousands!; sometimes it seems like the books are holding up the shelves. Let me paint you a picture of my terrible life. Every weekend we'd go the bookstore just to buy more books, then on Wednesdays we would go to the library and check out even more books. During all this book stuff I like to pretend I'm on an adventure taking all the books into outer space, dropping some off on each planet one by one. I start to think hmmm "what would the world be like without any books? "My name is Jared and I really hate books".

Sometimes when I'm outside having a little fun, my mom would call me to come inside to read. I can still hear her yelling out my name; "Jaareeed! Come in the house, it's time to read". I remember sitting on the edge of my bed with my hands covering my eyes, then my mother would walk in and say "Jared, do you want to read mother a story from one of your books"? I responded, "I hate reading". She replied, "one day you'll grow up and thank me for all this reading". I then jumped up and stood on top of bed. "One day I will fly like Superman and run faster than a train".

"What else will my little superhero do"? My mother asked. In the mist of it all I asked my mother if we could watch a superman movie. As she began to walk out the room she stopped and said, "Not now Jared, you don't have time to watch movies you need to read first". "Man do I hate books".

From the 2nd grade through second, I spent most of my time just reading and studying, not having much time for friends or playing. Sometimes my dad played catch with me, and the family would occasionally go out for fun, other times we would have game day. On the game days, my cousins, mostly around my age would come over to play. While there outside playing. my mom would have me inside reading, Once I completed reading a book, I would be able to go outside.So, I would read the quickest book I could find, yeaahhh you know what I'm thinking, "The Cat in The Hat" sounds nice. I should not, could not, would not continue to watch my cousins outside playing while I'm stuck inside with a book. So, I introduced myself to Dr. Seuss. With some quick flips of the pages, book complete, outside I went.

These were some of the more interesting times. After a long boring summer, school would begin soon.

Finally I made it to the 3rd grade. My teachers name is Mrs. Minjelly. At Lincoln Elementary, books were not my only problem. There was this kid named Travis, Travis Scott, a 5th grader. Although he was in the 5th grade, somehow he was in my class. He was one of the tallest kids in the school. Not only was he tall, he was also bulky, mean, and terrifying. He would bully most kids in the school and was known to not be very smart. During the 2nd grade I heard horror stories of him.

"Stay away from Travis" all the kids would say. I asked, "who is Travis"? the school bully they told me. Mikey, who I became friends with once told me that Travis put his dirty sock in a boys mouth so he couldn't talk and also took his lunch. Dyson, who I met though Mikey, whom everyone called "Pickles". I never knew why everyone called him "Pickles" until I witnessed how many pickles he would bring to school every day. Sometimes when you're close enough to him, he would reek of pickles. He also told me a story about what Travis did to another kid. The story goes during me during a recess Travis once threw a dodge ball into a kid's face and sent him to the hospital with a broken nose. Dyson also mentioned the kid never came back to school after that. There were several stories about Travis that rumored around the school. I couldn't believe he was in the 5th grade and couldn't read, maybe that's why he was a bully.

The school bell rings, Travis was waiting in the hallway for us. He lined up a few other 3rd graders and me against the lockers. He then yells out "Alright you little squirts, give me all your candy, lunch, and your lunch money." Mrs. Mingjellly would often give out candy to all the kids in class that made a good grade.

By Travis knowing this he would take full advantage and take it from us. They all began to give up their candy, lunch, and money. I just stood there in fright not giving him anything. I was next, he came up to me; "Jared, give up your candy, lunch, and money or you will regret it" he said. At that moment I don't know what came over me. With my heart pounding and wondering what to do next, out of my mouth came "I have something better, come follow me to the bathroom" I told him. He hesitated, "are you some type of weirdo" he said. "This better not be a trick Jared".

He grabs me by my shirt and pulled close,

"you better not waste my time-lets go." After he put all that stuff he took from we headed towards the bahroom. When we entered the bathroom, I reached into my backpack and pulled out a book about the solar system.

"Is this some sort of joke, does that look like candy or money to you" Travis said. He began balling his fist ready to punch me in the face. I didn't know what to say or do. In that brief moment, right before he could punch me, I held the book up square to his face and screamed out wait, wait! I began to tell him I overheard Mrs.Mingjelly telling another teacher that we will be having a pop quiz on Monday testing us on the planets, and solar system. Now you can have a head start on studying. He grabbed me by t-shirt and lifted me off my feet. "I can't read that well and; besides, I don't study Jared! you probably know this". Right then a light bulb came on in my head. I said to him, "Travis I can teach you how to read better and help you past the test so you can earn your own candy." He let loose of my shirt. After a quick stare he responded, "how do you think your going to do that"? I replied, "we can meet up after school in the library and study there". He paused briefly with a puzzled look on his face and to my surprise he agreed. Then he said, "Alright let's do it, but if I fail the test you won't have any teeth left". He pushes me against the wall and leaves the bathroom. I began to smile knowing my brilliance just saved me from a fate of the unknown. Now I just need to figure out how to keep my teeth.

During that next week, Travis and I continued to meet at the library. I must say being alone with Travis wasn't the easiest thing to do. Throughout that week I had to plan so my mom could allow me the extra time I needed after school. She wasn't aware I was meeting with a bully to teach him about the planets. By the following Monday it seemed like Travis was ready to pass the pop quiz, finally I could breathe a little, but I still had books waiting for me at home. On Monday, as we already knew, Mrs. Mingjelly was going surprised the class with the pop quiz. She started handing out the quizzes. I took a quick look over at Travis as he stared at me, with one of his fists imitating a punch in the teeth. I grew nervous not knowing what would happen. Throughout testing I would often look over at Travis to see what my chances were. Not one time did he look back up, he actually seemed focus.

Once the test was over, surprisingly Mrs.

Mingjelly handed out candy anyway rather we passed or not. When class was over, all of us started to rush out of class to get ahead of Travis. We all knew whom ever left after him would probably have given up their candy, lunch, and money because he would be waiting. I often wondered what Travis did with all that stuff. This time the teacher gave us a head start without knowing, because she had Travis wait to see her after class. I stood outside next to the lockers waiting for him to face my fate. Mikey seen me and asked if I was crazy to wait. "Don't you know you have a chance to get away from Travis", he said. I responded.

"I have something I must know". With nothing left to be said, Mikey and Dyson took off running down the hallway. So, after watching them run down the hallway, I looked behind me and Travis was there, right in my face. He looked like he was mad, so I closed my eyes, then I heard, "you're alright with me Jared". I thought I was dreaming. He put his hand on top my head and with excitement he said, "Jared I passed". I looked stunned and then he said, "If anyone messes with you come find me". Right then I knew that my days of getting bullied by Travis was over. Who knows, one day we might even be friends. Third grade had its challenges and 4th grade will most likely have more. For the rest, my 3rd grade school year I didn't have anymore problems out of Travis; I started to enjoy school a little more.

After my 3rd grade year, that summer my mom decided in my 4th grade year I could play little league baseball. For the first little league practice, coach Miles held a meeting with the parents and kids at our local park. All the boys were throwing the baseball back and forth, playing catch. I decided to put my glove on and join in. This kid named Tommy walks up to me, to welcome me to the team. He's been playing little league since the first grade, and all the kids called him "Cool Papa". He was the fastest kid on the team and he also threw a mean fast ball. My teammates told me if you're not ready for it, catching one of his fast balls could knock the wind out of you! It was said, Charlie, who is the catcher on the team, once got rushed to the hospital with a bruised hand for catching one of "Cool Papa's" fast pitch balls they called it.

While introducing myself to the team Charlie the catcher yells out, "hey you, aren't you that nerdy kid at school that is always on the playground reading"? Everyone started to laugh at me. I started walking away with my

glove on thinking this sport is not
for me. While I was walking away,
I heard "Cool Papa" calling my
name, "Jared! Jared!" I turned my
head to look back and seen a fast ball
speeding towards me. Instantly, I leaped
up in the air and caught the ball in my
left-hand glove with no problem. Once
I landed with ball in my glove,
all my teammates came running
towards me all excited saying,
"Jared caught "Cool
Papa's" fast

pitch ball with no problem at all!" They were cheering me on, calling me "Lefty".

They kept chanting, "Lefty, Lefty". I started to think, could I have learned the technique of catching fast balls from reading sports books all month?

I giggled and shook my head in doubt. No way, could a book help me do that? I did play catch with my dad sometimes, and I'm probably just gifted, I thought.

Practice was almost over; I was having so much fun I did not want to leave. That catch changed my life. After many practices, our first game was approaching, and the coach finally asked me to play left field for the remainder of the season. I was so excited. Before I left the final pre-season practice, I had to choose a jersey for the games, so I just reached in the box and pulled one out. I was lucky it was my size and it was the number seventy-three.

For the first time I felt like I fit in somewhere doing something other than reading, something else that could brighten my future. When I got in the car my mom reminded me, I had a test at in two weeks, so when I get home I needed to study. On the way home I asked, "mom, my birthday is tomorrow could we invite the team over to celebrate with me"? "No Jared she said,

not this time, I have something else planned for us to do".

On the day of my birthday I sat around in my room reading most of the day. Later that afternoon my mom came into my room. "Jared, I have a surprise for you she said, now close your eyes and count to three". I closed my eyes and began counting out loud as she walked me into the dining room. I had visions of my baseball team standing out front waiting for me with all types of presents. I started to get a little excited. My mom then tells me, "okay Jared you can open your eyes now".

When I opened my eyes, standing in front of me was mom, dad, and a few cousins. My mom was holding my birthday cake which was custom made to look like three big books and my dad and cousins were holding some gifts. On top of the cake was nine candles, of course I had to make a wish. I wished I wouldn't have to read anymore books for the rest of my life. Even though my team was not there I still had fun. I began to gain more friends through playing baseball.

I eventually became a star on the team. Some days we would have games in the rain. I could remember before baseball on rainy days I had to stay inside and read all day. Now I don't like rainy days. So, I decided on the rainy days to have fun with it, and it became my series day. I would pick some of my favorite series on those days; "Lord of Rings", "Harry Potter", "Nancy Drew Mysteries" were among some of the series I chose. I wanted to tell my mother that I would not, could not, and should not read any more books, but I was afraid she would just buy me more books and keep me in on sunny days. "Do I hate books?"

While in the 5th grade I began reading more advance books. My mom wanted me to challenge myself more, to get ahead of

the learning curve before I go to Junior high school. I was already reading at a high school level. I started to get more involved in classics and history books.

One day I was waiting for the bus to come, it was cold and windy outside. I went to sit under a nearby tree to get my jacket out of my backpack. I also took out the book my mom got me for my birthday, the book was called "M.C Higgins The Great" I started reading it and the next thing I knew, I was so into the book that the bus passed by without me realizing it. I had to go back home and ask my mom for a ride to school. As I was riding to school,

I sat in the backseat because I wanted to finish reading where I had left off, also I didn't want my mom to make a big deal out of me reading. I looked out the window to see why the car had stopped. I realized that we had made it to school. I looked up towards the rear-view mirror and saw my mother. She was just staring at me with tears in her eyes and a big smile.

For some reason she was just smiling like she never had before. I could not believe it— that day her face really did light up! I thought to myself "was this all just a test"? Did I realize my life lesson? Was she waiting for this moment my whole life? Or was it something

else? All these questions came over me, but

I had no answer. Though it was cold that day,

I got a warm and fuzzy feeling all over.

I grabbed my backpack and book, and then

I got out of the car. I just stood there for a

moment waiting for my mom to drive off.

She rolled down the window and called me over

to the car. I leaned in to see what she wanted,

and I noticed that on the seat was a book

entitled "Helping Your Child Love to Read".

I thought to myself, I get now. At that

moment I knew my mother was not one of

those parents who tell their children to read

constantly but the parents never pick up a book for themselves. I realized mom must enjoy reading too. It just took me a while to realize reading wasn't so bad.

Will I worry about my mom buying me more books because she thinks I enjoyed reading so much? Yes, of course I will. But I wouldn't trade that moment for anything in the world. I started walking to class, smiling and holding my book "M.C Higgins" proudly in my hand. Now that I have more friends, reading books and school became more tolerable. I often think of Travis because he moved on to junior High school a couple years back. Next year I will be in Junior High school. Maybe I will see Travis, and we would still be friends. It was the final days of the school year and my 5th grade graduation was approaching. I was excited about graduation. I was worried my mother would not be able to attend due to an important business trip she had that weekend. My father assured me that she would not miss it for anything in the world.

The morning of my graduation I woke up ready and refreshed with a hint of worry. While at school I did not see my mother in the crowd. The principle asked all fifth graders to stand and line up. They began to call names;

one by one we crossed the stage. When my turn came, I took a deep breath and closed my eyes. I began to think I froze for a second— how could I have made it this far without my mother pushing me to read every day? Now, in one of my greatest moments, she will not see me walk across the stage. I felt my hands getting sweaty and my eyes began to water. You know that uncomfortable feeling you get in the bottom of your stomach, it was there. Suddenly, I heard a loud scream; Seventy-three!

I thought to myself, that's my baseball number! I smiled even though I could not see her, I knew she was there. As I walked across the stage, I continued to hear the cheers of my name and number coming from my family in the crowd.

Even though I didn't like reading it gave me that confidence that I could conquer the world. I was ready and prepared for the next chapter in my life. At the end of graduation while standing there with my mom, dad, and family I felt a tap on my shoulder. When I looked to see who it was. It was Travis. He reached out to shack my hand then He said to me, "congratulations Jared, how about this summer let me introduce you to who I hang with."

As he walked away, he turned back and yelled "Welcome to Junior High school"! My mother gave me great big hug and asked, "are you ready for Junior high school Jared?" I replied, "Is Junior high school ready for me"? My mother's theory holds true, she once told me after reading over a thousand books you will have the world at your fingertips. Ready or not world. Here I come.

Hi, remember me?

My name is Jared, and books are not so bad!

CPSIA information can be obtained
at www.ICGtesting.com
Printed in the USA
LVHW071355190121
676877LV00015B/533

9 781087 933719